Map of the Kaaterskill Clove

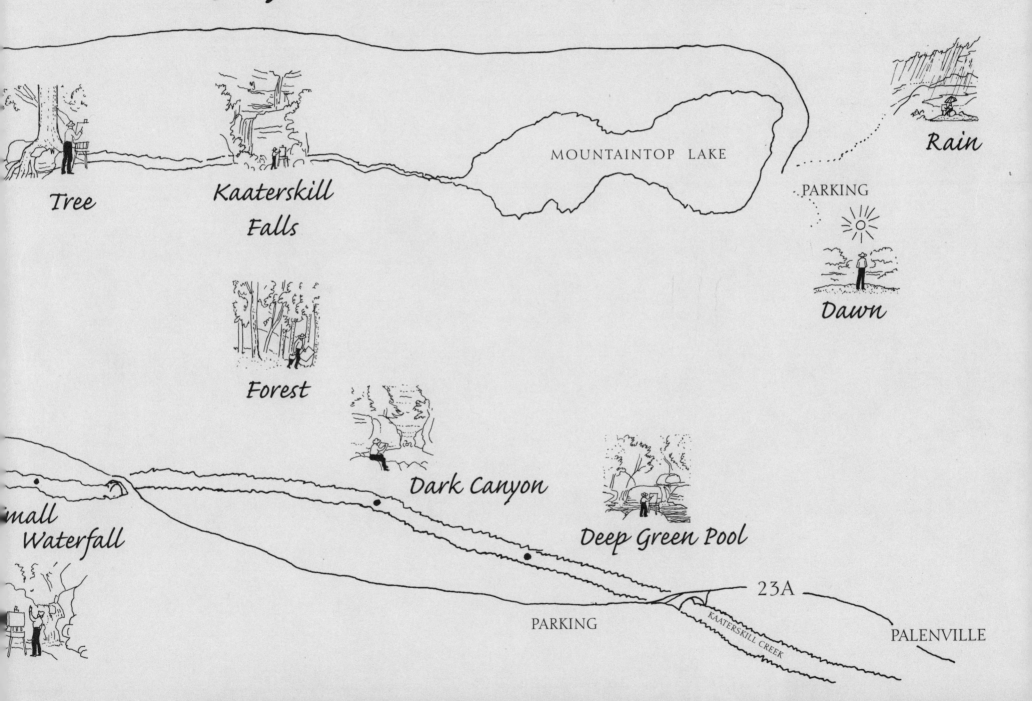

AN ARTIST'S RETURN TO AMERICA'S FIRST WILDERNESS

In Blue Mountains

AN ARTIST'S RETURN TO AMERICA'S FIRST WILDERNESS

In Blue Mountains

Thomas Locker

BELL POND
BOOKS

Hudson, New York

Friends of my heart, lovers of nature's works,

Let me transport you to those wild, blue mountains

That rear their summits near the Hudson's waves.

Though not the loftiest that begirt the land,

They yet sublimely rise, and on their heights

    your soul may have a sweet foretaste of heaven ....

        — Thomas Cole, "The Wild"

Deep in American consciousness lies a memory of the place where the American vision of nature began. In the Hudson River valley of upstate New York there is a gorge that many call "America's first wilderness." Its name is the Kaaterskill Clove. Here Washington Irving set one of the first works of American literature, his story *Rip Van Winkle*. A few years later, it was the subject of the first truly American landscape, painted by Thomas Cole, the founder of the Hudson River School of painters.

As a small boy I, too, experienced the beauty of nature for the first time in the Kaaterskill Clove. That childhood experience perhaps explains why, as a young art student, I began to learn how to paint landscapes in the style of the Hudson River School. I did not think much about this, however, until I returned to the Clove in 1987 to complete sketches for a Rip Van Winkle picture book. When I did those paintings, I fell in love with the landscapes of the Clove for the second time. And so, to be near them, I moved to the little village of Stuyvesant, just across the river from the Catskill Mountains.

Since then I have spent many summers painting the mountains and hiking in them with friends. Some of these friends are naturalists, biologists, chemists, and historians. Through their eyes and thoughts I began to see the "first wilderness" of the Hudson River valley through scientifically-oriented, twentieth-century eyes.

Faced with a serious medical problem and recognizing my own mortality, I turned to the Clove with a new sense of purpose in 1997. I fell in love with it for the third time — in a new way. I felt a need to clarify my own way of seeing nature.

The paintings in this book are the result of this vision quest. The children's story and the notes at the back are my attempt to bring together, for young and old alike, a lifetime's involvement with this special place. The Kaaterskill Clove has helped me to see the beauty of the natural world. A recognition of beauty is often the first step in falling in love. I hope that this book will help others to love the world.

THOMAS LOCKER

Once there was an artist who loved to sit on a hillside, painting pictures of the pale blue mountains in the distance. He painted them so often that he knew their outlines by heart. Year after year, they inspired him. People loved his pictures, and he sold everything he painted. But, one day, he realized his pictures were not getting any better. "Perhaps my work would improve," he thought, "if instead of always painting the mountains from a distance, I were to spend the summer painting deep inside them." And that is what he did. He followed the river across the valley and, by nightfall, found lodging at the foot of the blue mountains, at the edge of the wilderness.

The very first morning he found a stream plunging into a deep, green pool. "I'll paint exactly what I see," he decided. So he took out his pencil and began to draw. He tried to draw all the trees with their millions of leaves. He drew and drew and drew until his whole canvas was a jumble of tiny lines. "This is going nowhere," he said. "I could draw leaves all summer and never draw them all. There must be another way." So he took out his paints and brushes, and painted the big shapes and colors. Then he added just enough detail to capture the feeling of the place. Finally, he stepped back and looked at his picture. "Painting wilderness is a real challenge," he thought. "I will try again tomorrow."

Next day, he followed the stream into a deep gorge.
He was feeling very confident. His confidence, however,
did not last, for he quickly discovered that there was very
little light in the gorge. All morning he struggled to paint
the half light of the shadows. He just couldn't do it.
His picture looked dull and grey. He was about to give up!
Then, at midday, the sun shone down into the gorge.
The rock walls suddenly sparkled in the brilliant light.
Now, when he painted the bright, rose-colored walls,
the shadows in his painting looked right! So he had
learned something. "If I want to capture deep shadows,
I have to paint bright light," he said.

Things became difficult again when he started painting a picture of a small waterfall hidden in the forest. Day after day, he came back to work on it. But it never looked right. The reds clashed with the greens. The water looked white and lifeless. "This is too hard," he sighed. A bluefly buzzed over his head. He looked up. Yellow-green light was streaming through the leaves. "Aha!" he said. He mixed up some yellow-green paint. Then he added the yellow-green to everything. His painting looked much better. "I see," he said, "the light coming through the leaves changes the color of everything."

The artist was worn out after his struggle to paint the gorge. He felt like going back to paint the mountains from the distance. It was time to take a break. He decided to pack a lunch and go for a long walk. When he came to a clearing, he stopped and looked out at the sky. He had missed the sky while he was in the gorge. He sat down against a tree and ate his sandwich. The mountains on both sides were like waves of flowing water. It was very peaceful. That night, he dreamed of the view from the clearing. When he awoke, he decided to stay in the mountains. So he went back to the clearing with his paints and brushes. This time, he finished his picture so quickly that there was time left to start another one.

One day, the artist found a huge, moss-covered rock, built up in layers like a fancy cake. It must have weighed at least a thousand tons! As he began to paint, he noticed that the stream had washed away the earth beneath the rock. Sooner or later it would tumble down the mountainside. The artist hoped no one would be in the way! "Everything is changing all the time," he thought. "I can't paint that. I can paint only what I see." Then he painted the light bouncing off the top of the rock, while the stream gurgled away beside him.

Near the rock stood an ancient hemlock tree. Its roots clawed into the earth, its trunk reached into the sky. He wanted to paint it. "How can a tree live on top of a rock?" he wondered. "There must have been soil here when the tree was little. Perhaps the stream carried the soil away. Maybe the stream even dug this whole gorge." Then, in his painting, he tried to capture the sense that everything is connected. As he did, he could hear the sound of water falling.

When he saw it, the waterfall took his breath away. It was so tall that the artist couldn't see the top without arching his neck. When he looked at the bottom, he could see only halfway up. How could he possibly paint it all? He closed his eyes and imagined what it would look like if he could see it whole. "Wilderness is too big to see the whole of it anywhere except in my imagination," he said. Then he turned back to his easel and painted what he saw in his imagination.

The artist wondered where the water flowing over the falls came from. He climbed up through the forest until he came to an opening in the trees. He looked out. Below him lay a little mountaintop lake, reflecting the sky. A drop of rain fell on his cheek. It began to pour. The artist set up his umbrella and painted the sheets of rain sweeping across the mountains. He could see the lake receiving the gifts of the sky. "Nature is being washed clean," he thought.

The nights were growing cooler now. The first hints of fall could be seen in the color of the leaves. One starry night, the artist camped out in a mountainside meadow. He awoke before dawn, covered with morning dew, and looked down into the valley at the river flowing toward the sea. As the sun rose, the clouds filled with water. "Nature moves in circles," he thought. "Round and round. Dawn is the end of night and the beginning of day." Then rose-yellow light slowly bathed everything. The sun rose over the horizon and the song of birds broke the silence.

Summer was almost over. There was time left to paint one last picture. The artist walked until he found a sweet-smelling forest. Now he knew what to do. He started with the big shapes and colors; then he put in the details. He thanked the bright light that helped him paint the shadows. He thanked the leaves that gave color to the forest light. He thanked the trees, rocks, water, and air. Most of all, he thanked the wilderness for teaching him to see in a new way.

On the last day of summer, the artist returned
once again to the hillside where his journey began.
He looked at the blue mountains with new eyes.
Now, he felt he could go on painting them forever.
Light touched the edge of a sunset cloud. His heart
was filled with the beauty of the world.

ABOUT BLUE MOUNTAINS

HOW WERE THE PAINTINGS IN THIS BOOK CREATED?

Like the nineteenth-century Hudson River painters, I spent several days making drawings and color sketches at each spot in the Kaaterskill Clove I wanted to paint. I took these sketches back to my studio and let time, memory, and dreams work their magic and sort out the important aspects of each site.

Using a red-toned canvas, I then worked out the big areas of light and dark, using white and dark brown paint. When this dried, I put on the colors in broad areas, saving the details for last.

Some oil paints become transparent when mixed with oil. You can then see through the paint to the paint below. When the undercolors are dry, I put on a transparent layer, called a *glaze*. Then I add the highlights into the wet glaze.

HOW LONG DID IT TAKE TO MAKE THESE PAINTINGS?

Not counting the days spent in nature making the drawing and color sketches, it takes three or four days to complete a picture. But I have had fifty years of practice. It really takes a lifetime to do each painting!

HOW WERE THE MOUNTAINS FORMED?

My geologist friends explain that mountains can be formed in several ways. Sometimes molten stone can push up from deep inside the earth to create volcanic mountains. Sometimes parts of the earth's surface, which is always moving, can push against another part to lift or fold the land.

The blue mountains are different.

Millions of years ago, there were snow capped peaks, higher than the Alps or the Rockies. But they were in another place — east of where they are now. In the course of time, wind and water wore them down. Then, streams carrying dissolved stone flowed into the ocean, forming a delta under the water. As the earth grew warmer, the ocean dried up, and the land rose to become a plateau. The delta, now the Catskill Mountains, was on top! In a miraculous process, wind and water still continue their work, carving the delta that was laid down in layers "like a fancy cake."

WHY DO ARTISTS PAINT DISTANT MOUNTAINS BLUE?

People often wonder why I keep painting pictures of the Catskills seen from a distance. One of the reasons is that they are never the same. When I look at the dark shapes of the mountains through water vapor and other parts of the atmosphere, they look sometimes grey and sometimes blue. The thicker the atmosphere, the paler the mountains appear. In the far distance, looking through miles of atmosphere, they seem very pale indeed.

A scientist friend once explained that the color of the mountains can be explained by the scattering of light as it bounces off particles in the atmosphere. Water vapor scatters the blue part of the spectrum. My friend added that modern physics and quantum mechanics cannot really define light or say with certainty whether it is a wave or a particle. Light is still a mystery and marvellous to paint.

HOW CAN A HEMLOCK TREE LIVE ON TOP OF A ROCK?

Everything in nature is connected and part of a single process. When the hemlock tree was born, about two hundred and fifty years ago, soil covered the rocks. So it took root, sending down its roots through the soil to the rock beneath. Because the roots produce an acid that can dissolve stone, the tree kept on growing, thrusting its roots through the rock! Taking food and water from whatever soil it could find, the hemlock was able to draw them up into its trunk, branches, and leaves. The hemlock tree releases water and gives off oxygen, helping to create the air we breathe. Everything — the rocks, the soil, the trees, the stream — are part of a connected process.

WHERE DOES THE WATER COME FROM THAT FILLS THE MOUNTAINTOP LAKES?

Some of the water comes from rain and snow, but most of the water comes from underground springs that rise upward, against the pull of gravity. The weight of the mountain pushes down on the water and puts it under pressure. The water then finds it way up through little crevices and becomes mountaintop springs. The huge root system of the surrounding forests helps "prime the pump" and helps to fill the lakes with water. There is a lot of water — many lakes and streams. Water from the Catskill Mountains provides New York City with most of its water supply! This shows us how much we depend on nature — we are part of the process. When we change nature we change ourselves.

WHAT KIND OF PEOPLE HAVE LIVED IN THE CATSKILLS?

For thousands of years, Native Americans were part of life in the Hudson River valley. They hunted and fished. The women planted gardens in forest clearings. When the garden lost its fertility, they moved it to another clearing. The men set fires in the forest to burn the underbrush, which made the hunting easier. Living in this way, the valley sustained a way of life. Historians estimate that about 10,000 native people were living in the valley when the Europeans arrived.

The first Europeans described the valley as a "wasteland." They quickly cut down the forest to create farms and villages. By the nineteenth century, people had enough leisure time to enjoy the arts. Poets and painters came to the valley, and the Clove became an important center of the nineteenth-century American art scene. America's first "nature tourists" stayed in hotels on the mountaintops. Gradually, however, the hotels went out of business. Two-and-a-half million people now live in the Hudson River valley, and the Clove is part of a state park, used by skiers, hikers, and a few year-round residents.

ARE THE PLACES IN THIS BOOK REAL?

If you follow the map, you will find the places illustrated in this book. You can stand in the places where landscape painters have stood since the start of American landscape painting. You can look out upon the nature they saw. Perhaps you will want to paint pictures of the way you see it.

WHY DO ARTISTS PAINT THE WILDERNESS?

America's first landscape painters went to the wilderness to be closer to God. For them, the wilderness was God's "untouched creation," and they studied design in nature to understand the divine designer. They loved beauty and what they called "the sublime."

When they saw balance and harmony in nature that reminded them of classical European paintings, they called it "beautiful." And when they experienced nature's overpowering force — in intense contrasts, unexpected lines, and dizzying heights — they described it as "sublime." They defined the sublime as "terror recollected in tranquillity."

When I returned to America's first wilderness, I didn't experience it in terms of terror. For me, it was a safe haven from the horrors of modern life. At first, I wandered through the Clove as through the ruins of an abandoned church where an almost forgotten religion had once been practiced. I could no longer see nature the way the nineteenth-century painters had seen it, but with my more scientifically-oriented twentieth-century eyes, I began to see it in a new way — as a complex, interrelated process.

It was while painting the Kaaterskill Falls that I realized, like the artist in the story, that nature is too great and vast to be understood by studying it part by part. For a painter, the only way to see nature as a whole is in the mind's eye, in an act of creative imagination and identification with nature. And so, when I found the wilderness within myself, its beauty filled my soul.

Now I wonder if the joy I experience in the Clove is really different from the experience of America's first landscape painters!

POSTSCRIPT

I hope IN BLUE MOUNTAINS will encourage you and your children to visit America's first wilderness,

or at least a wilderness close to your home. The beauty of the Clove — the beauty of nature everywhere — helps children love the world.

And love of the world, I believe, is fundamental to its preservation.

If you follow the map to the Clove to see it with your own eyes, you might well find me there.

I'll be that old man trying to paint the water flowing over the Kaaterskill Falls.

DEDICATED TO KAREN & NELSON

Acknowledgments first to Christopher Bamford without whom this book could not have been possible.
Nanette Stevenson for her guidance; Craig Holdrege, Director of The Nature Institute, for biological information;
Alf Evers, historian of the Catskills; Dr. Fisher, New York state geologist, retired, for checking geological information;
Mary Giddens for design.

The illustrations in this book were done in oils on canvas.
The text type is Goudy Old Style. The display type is Benguiat.

Printed by Phoenix Color Corp., New York/Maryland/Connecticut

Library of Congress Cataloging-in-Publication Data

Locker, Thomas, 1937-
    In blue mountains : an artist's return to America's first
wilderness / [story and paintings by] Thomas Locker. -- 1st ed.
    Summary: Painting landscapes of Kaaterskill Clove, a gorge
in the Hudson River Valley of upstate New York, helps an artist
discover the beauty of nature.
    ISBN 0-88010-471-6
    [1. Painting Fiction. 2. Artists Fiction. 3. Nature Fiction.
 4. Kaaterskill Clove (N.Y.) Fiction.]   I. Title.
PZ7.L7945In   2000
[Fic]--dc21   99-40197
                                                                     CIP

PRINTED IN THE USA   First edition   10 9 8 7 6 5 4 3 2 1

3-01

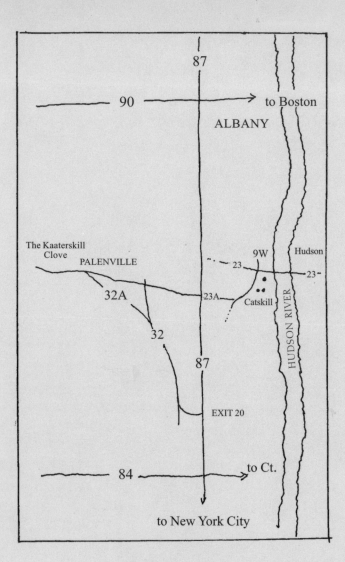

DISTANCES:

from New York City .... 105 miles

from Boston ....150 miles

from Albany .... 38 miles

from Catskill .... 8 miles

(as the crow flys)

Distant views of the mountains were painted
from hillsides in the village of Catskill.

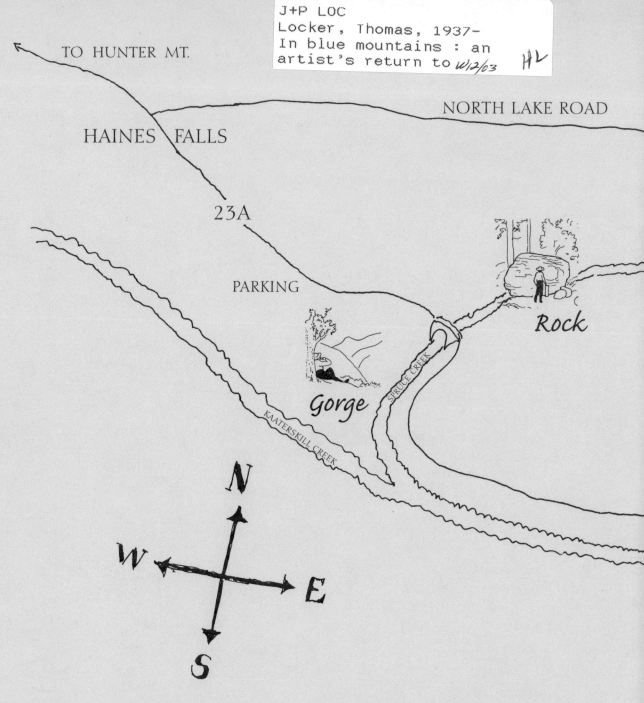

TO HUNTER MT.

NORTH LAKE ROAD

HAINES FALLS

23A

PARKING

Rock

Gorge

SPRUCE CREEK

KAATERSKILL CREEK

N
W   E
S